A Tony Millionaire Sock Monkey Adventure

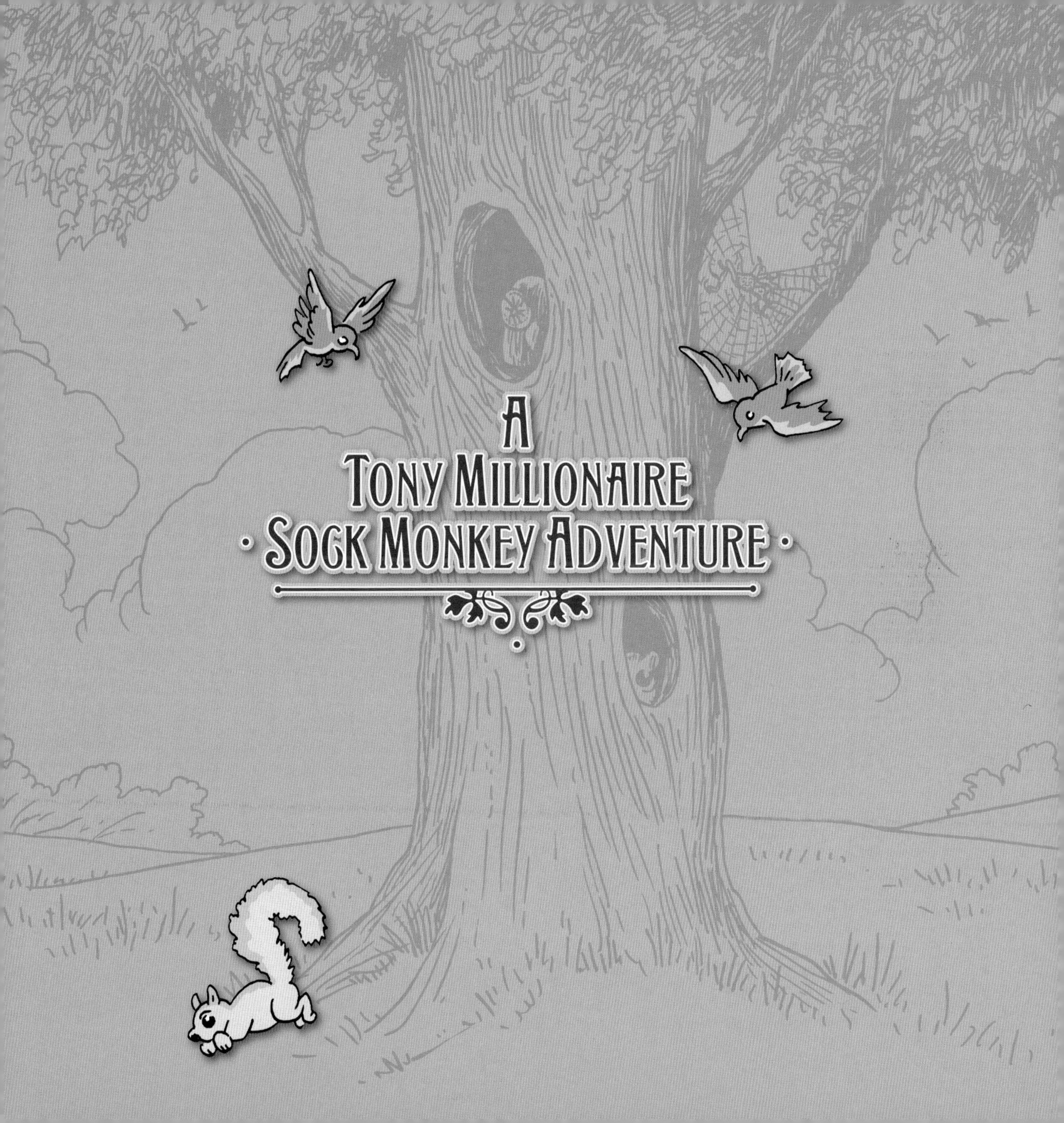

For Nancy

Little and Large

Tony Millionaire

DH Press™

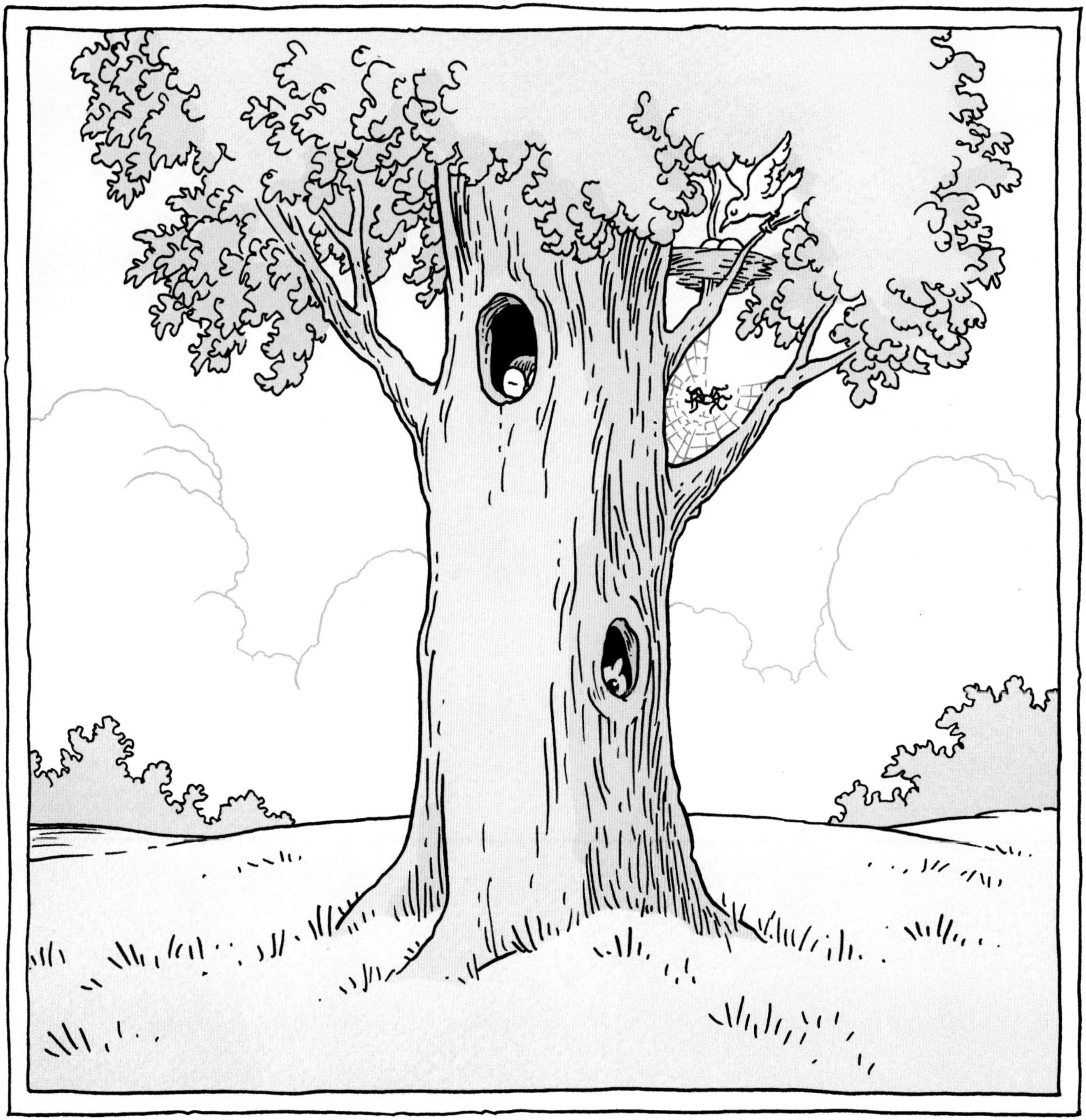

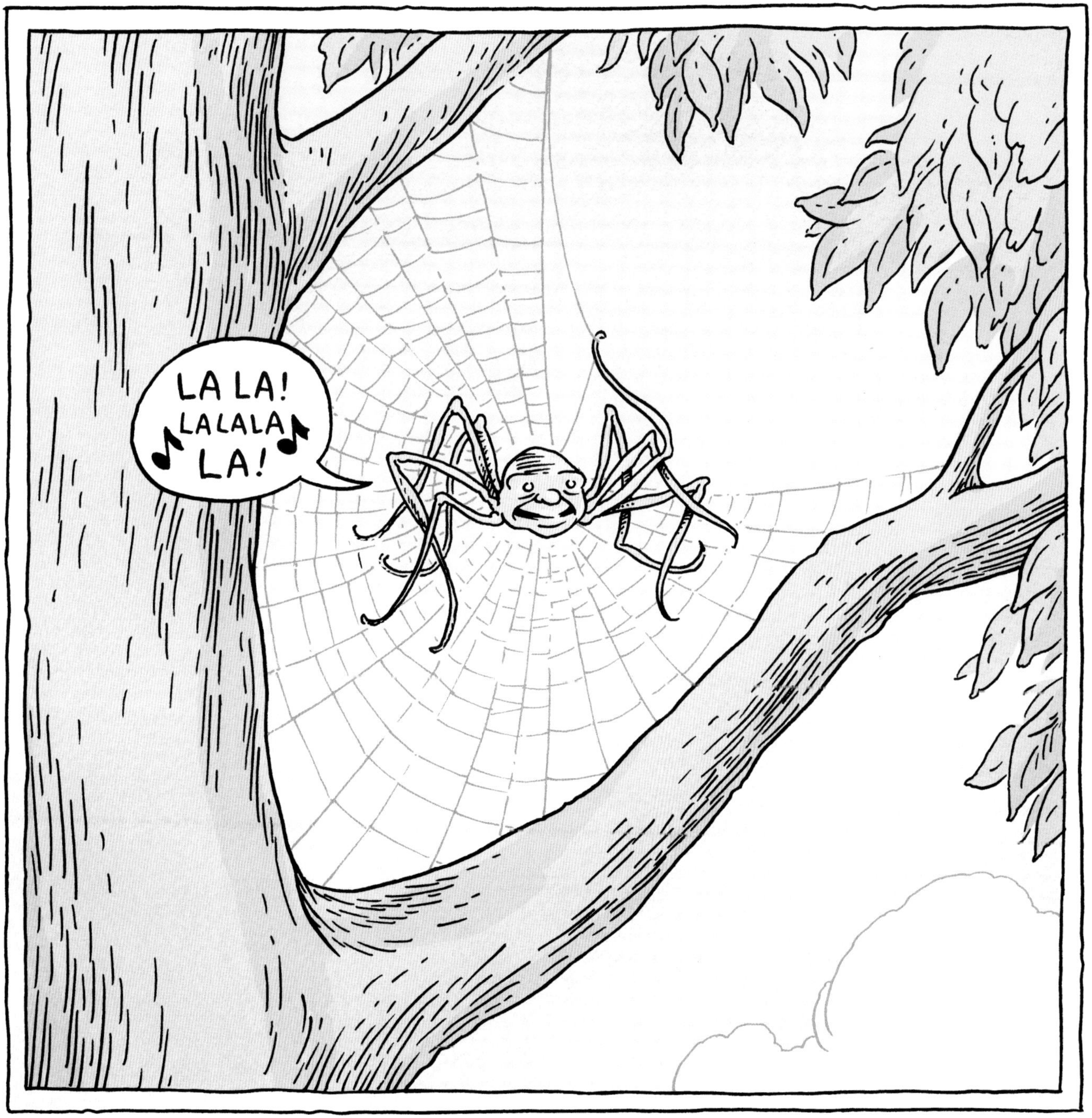
LA LA! LALALA LA!

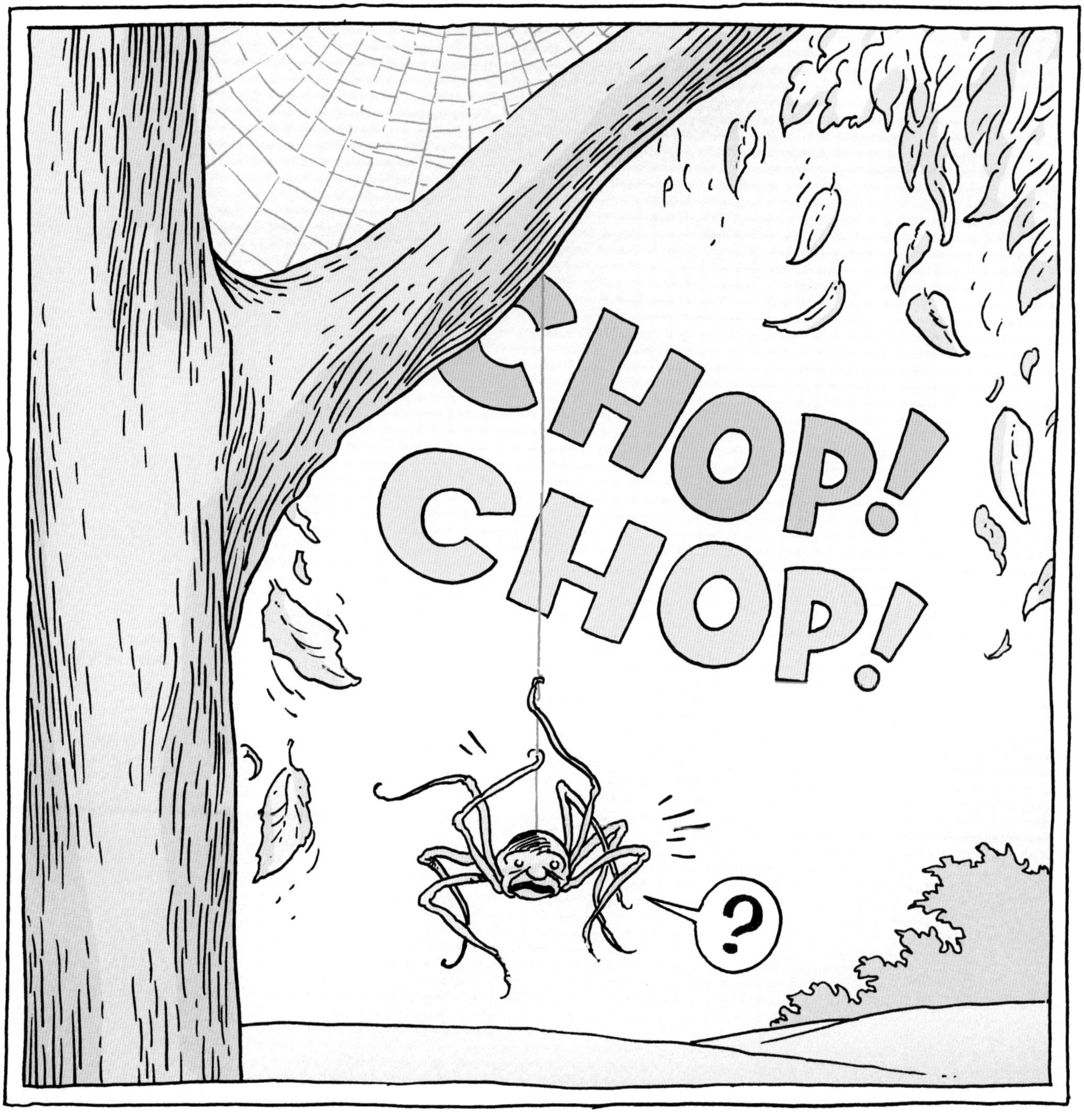
CHOP! CHOP!
?

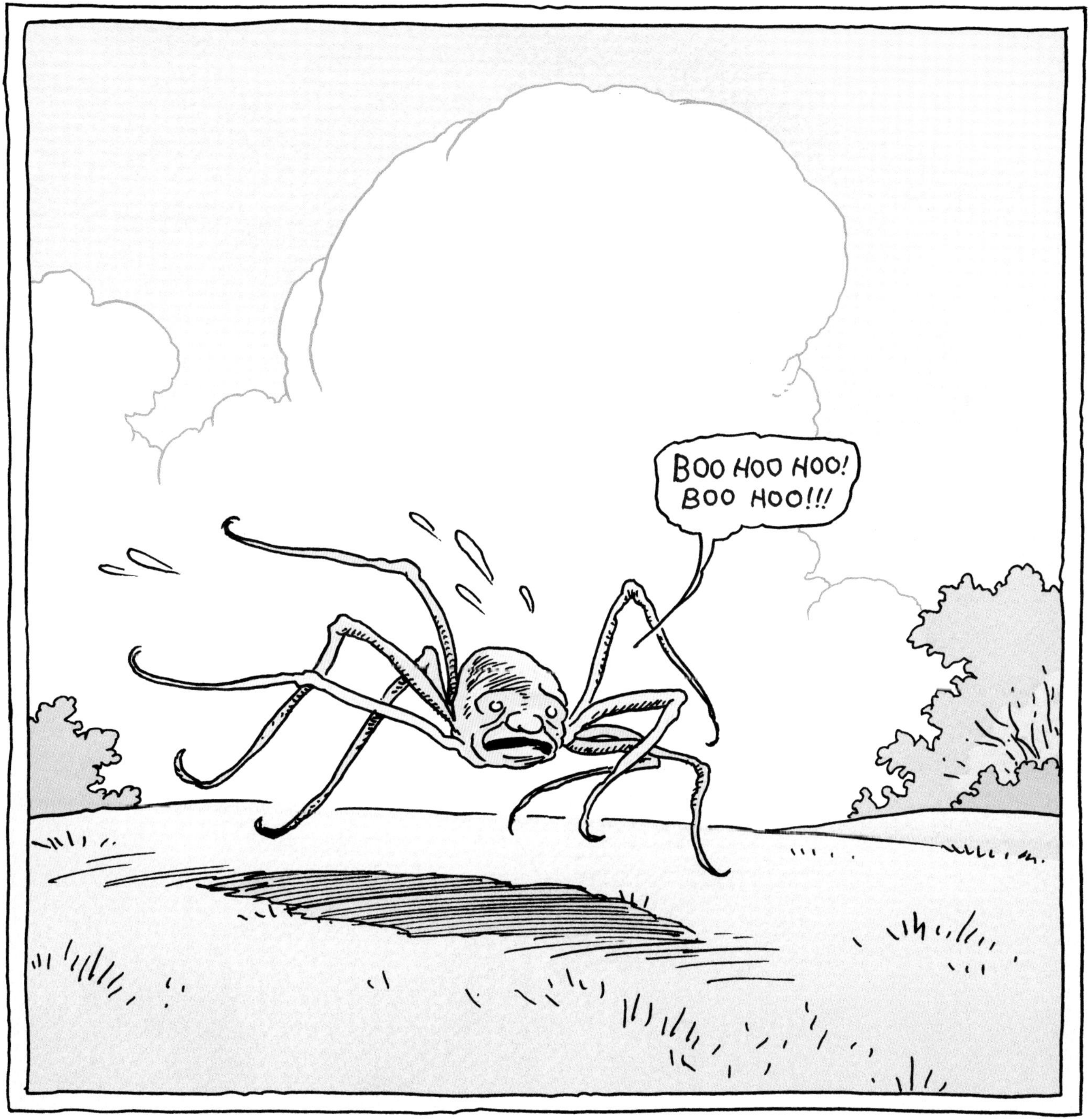
BOO HOO HOO! BOO HOO!!!

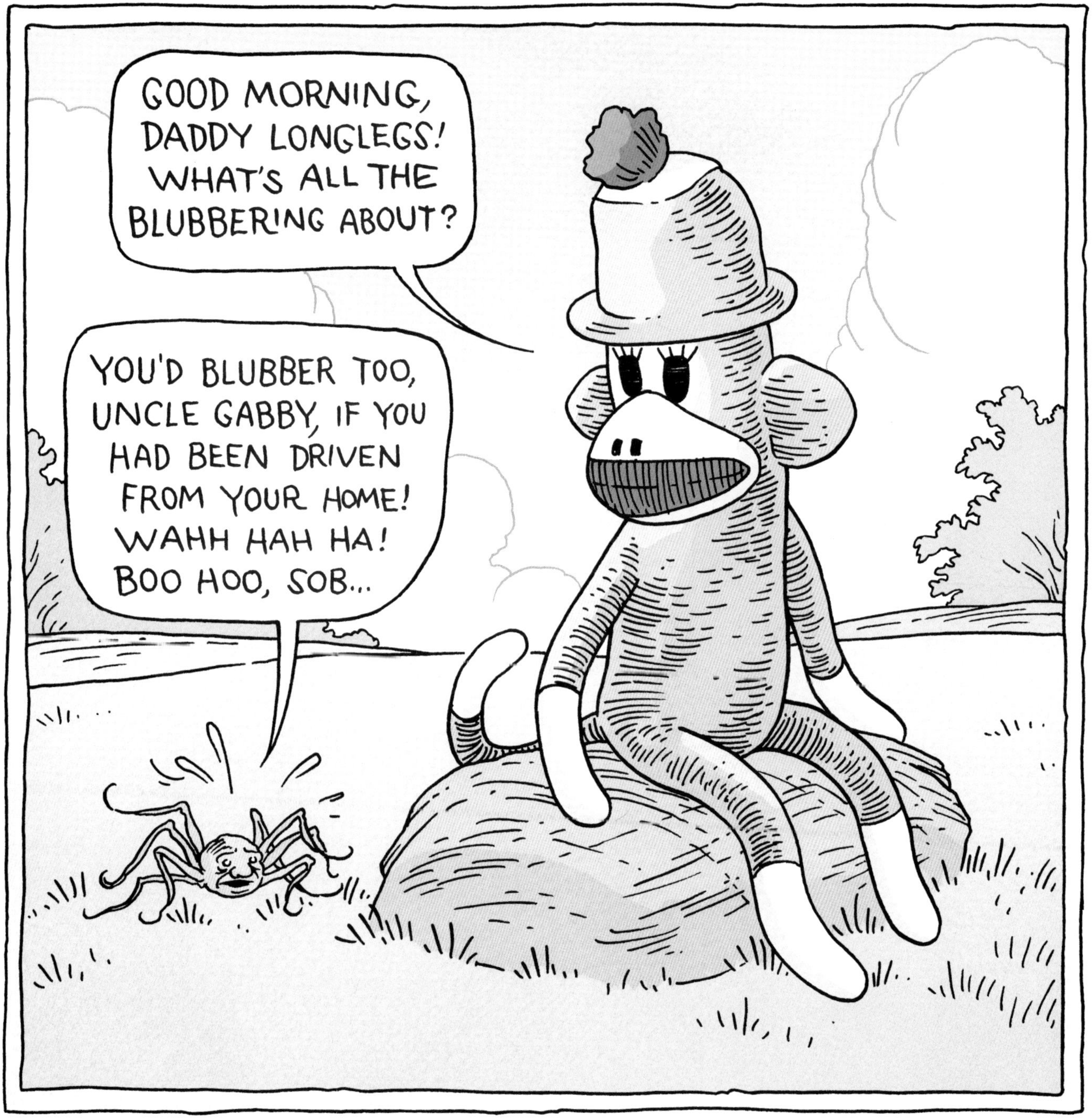
GOOD MORNING, DADDY LONGLEGS! WHAT'S ALL THE BLUBBERING ABOUT?
YOU'D BLUBBER TOO, UNCLE GABBY, IF YOU HAD BEEN DRIVEN FROM YOUR HOME! WAHH HAH HA! BOO HOO, SOB...

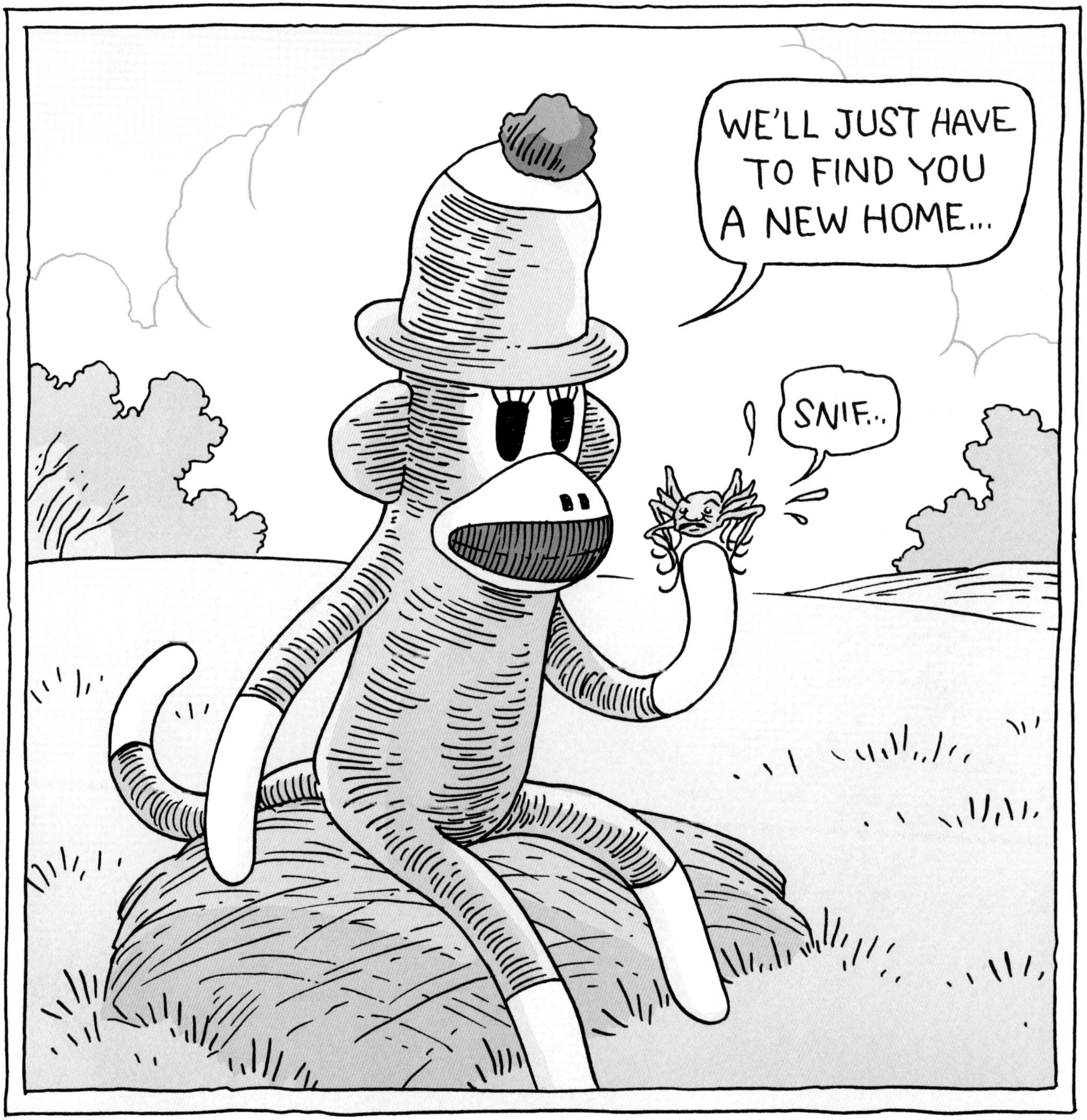
WE'LL JUST HAVE TO FIND YOU A NEW HOME...
SNIF..

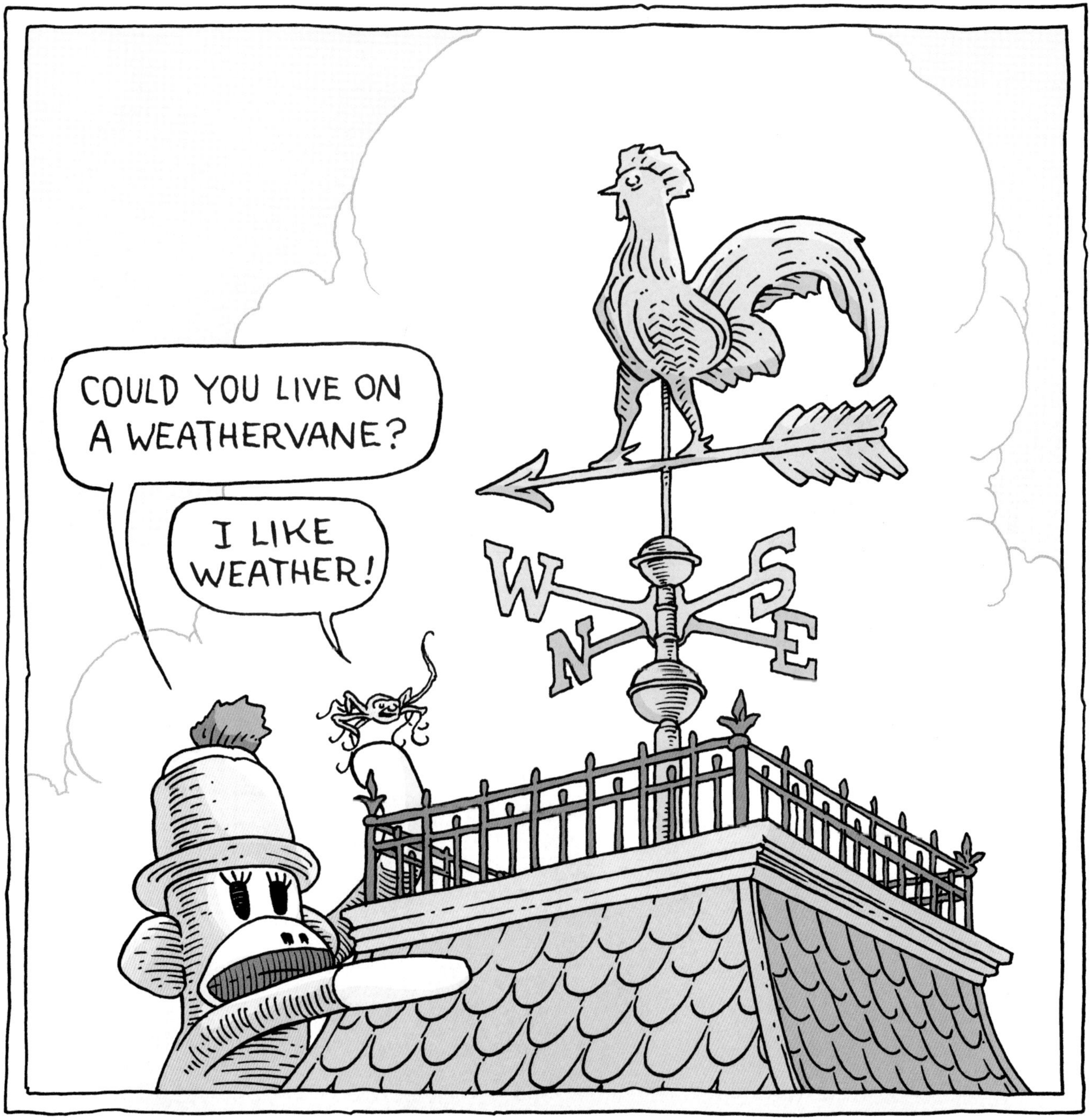
COULD YOU LIVE ON A WEATHERVANE?
I LIKE WEATHER!
W
S
N
E

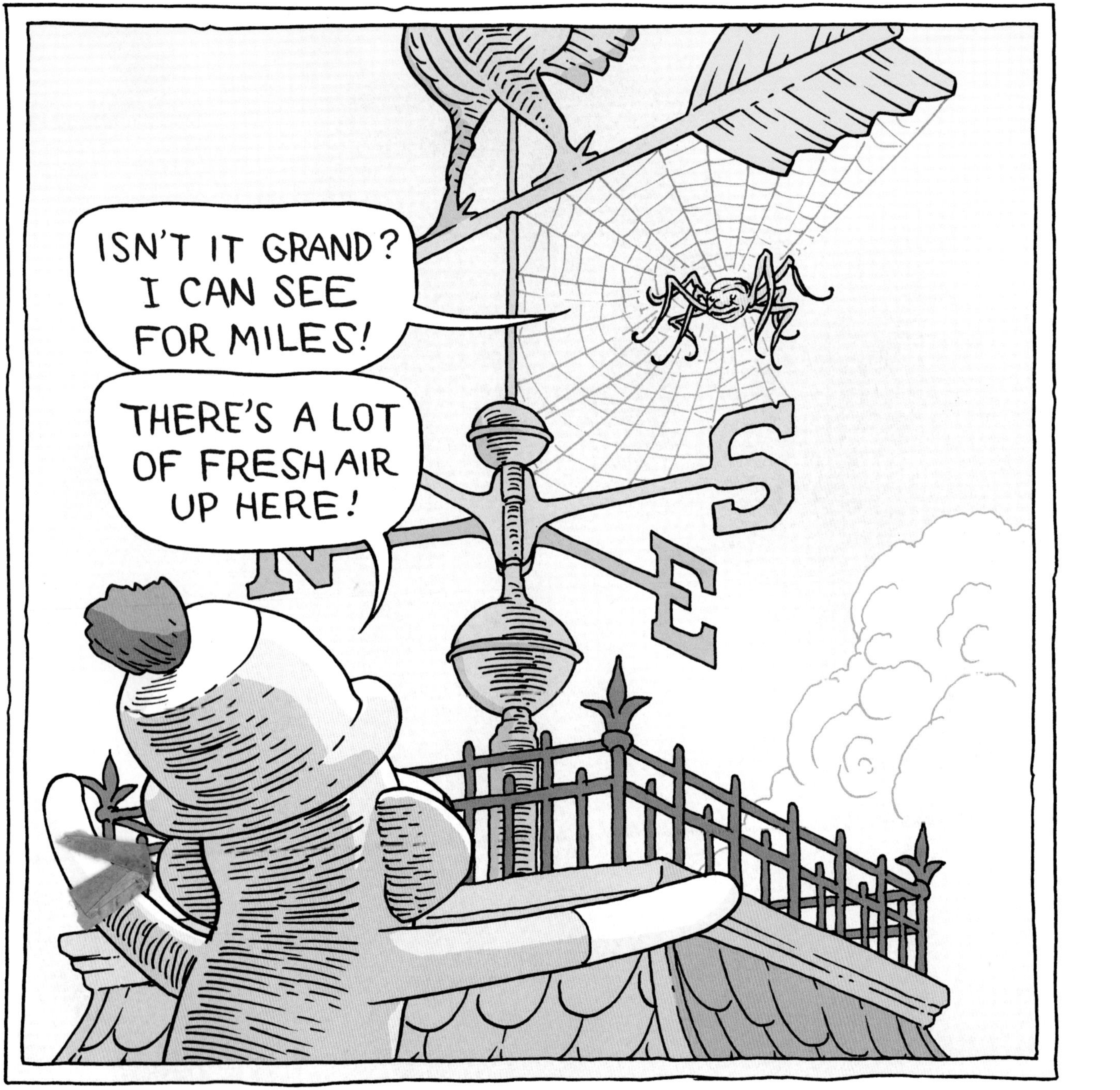
ISN'T IT GRAND? I CAN SEE FOR MILES!
THERE'S A LOT OF FRESH AIR UP HERE!
N
S
E

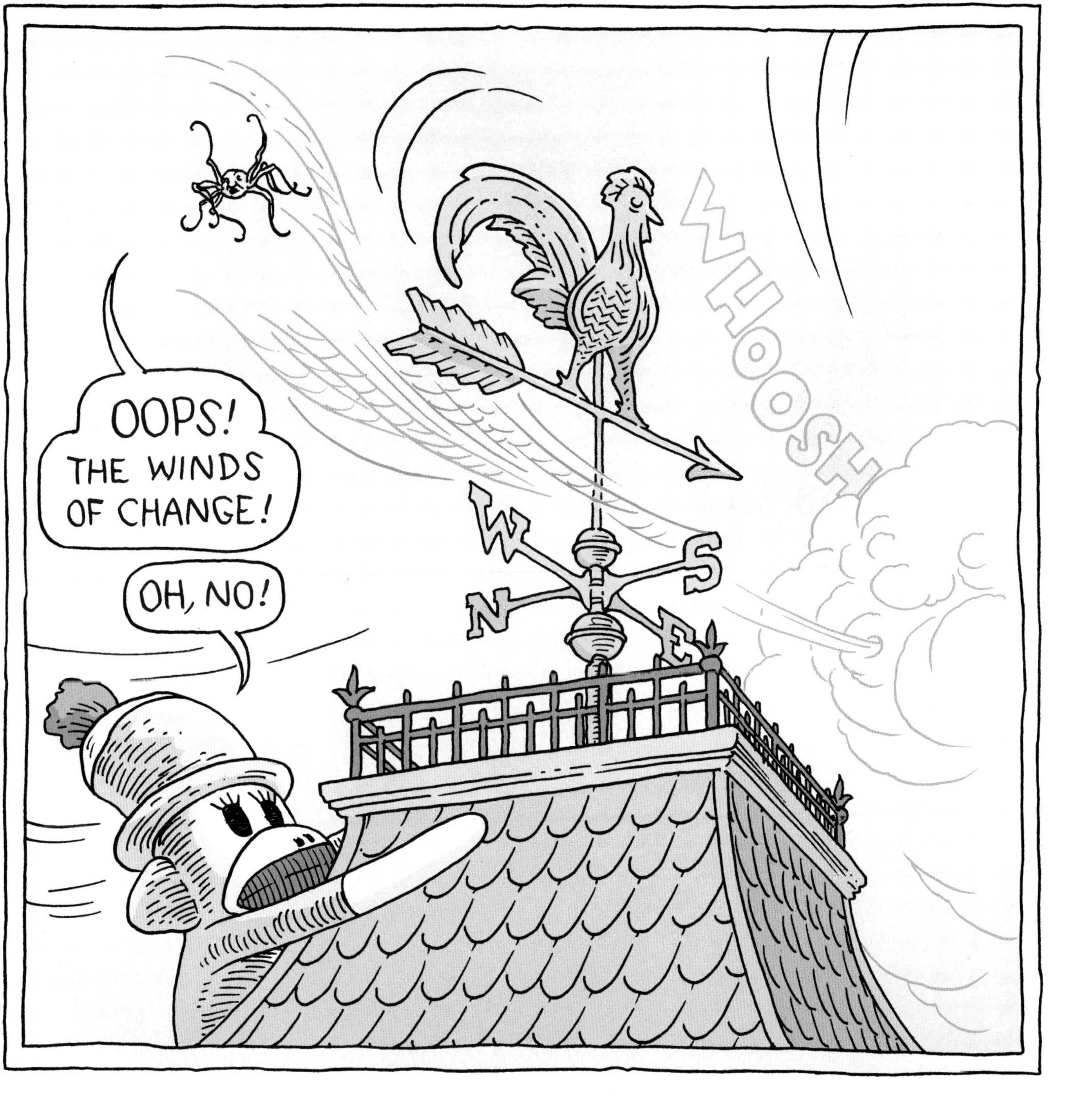
OOPS! THE WINDS OF CHANGE!
OH, NO!
WHOOSH
W
S
N
E

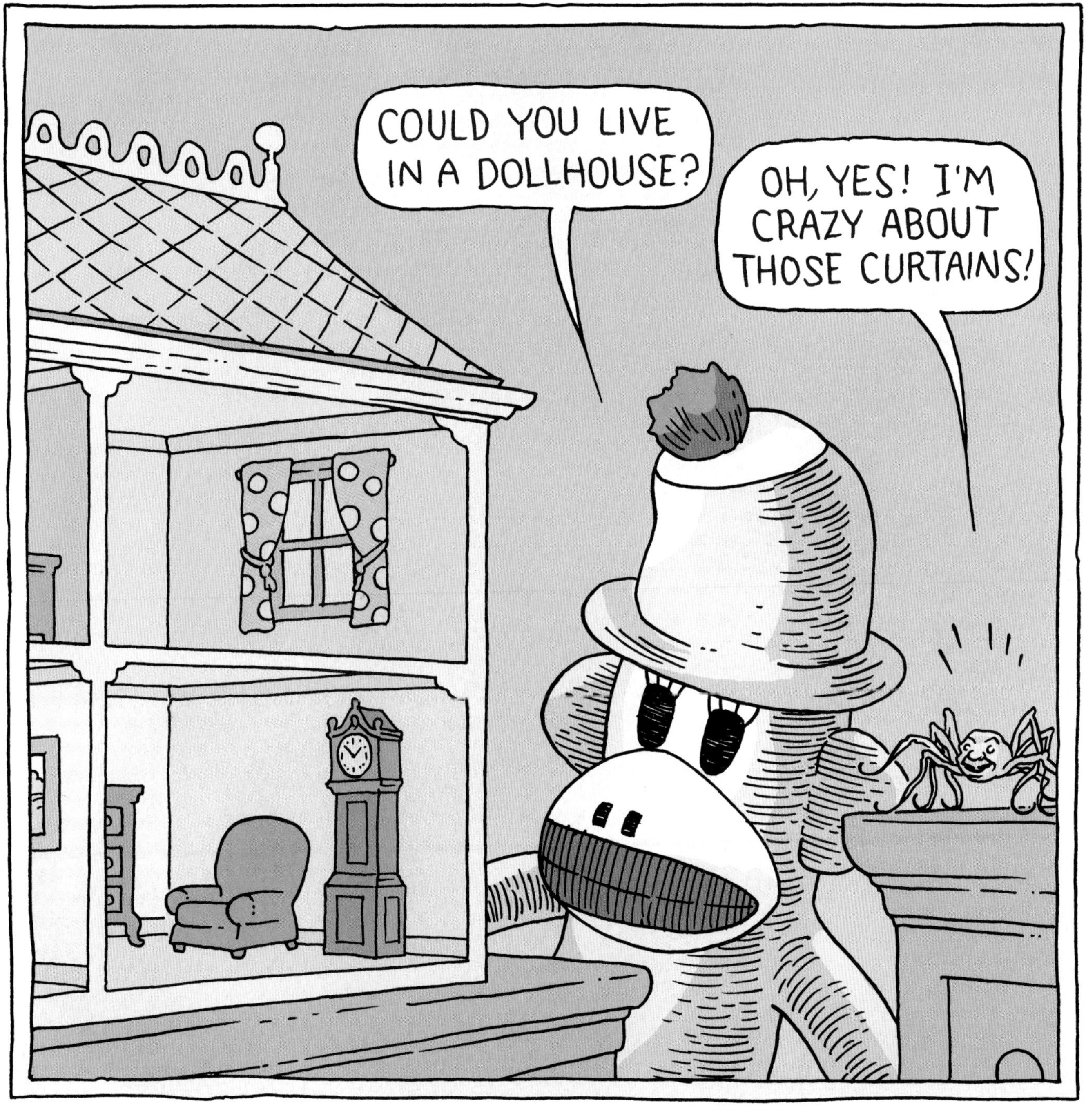
COULD YOU LIVE IN A DOLLHOUSE?
OH, YES! I'M CRAZY ABOUT THOSE CURTAINS!

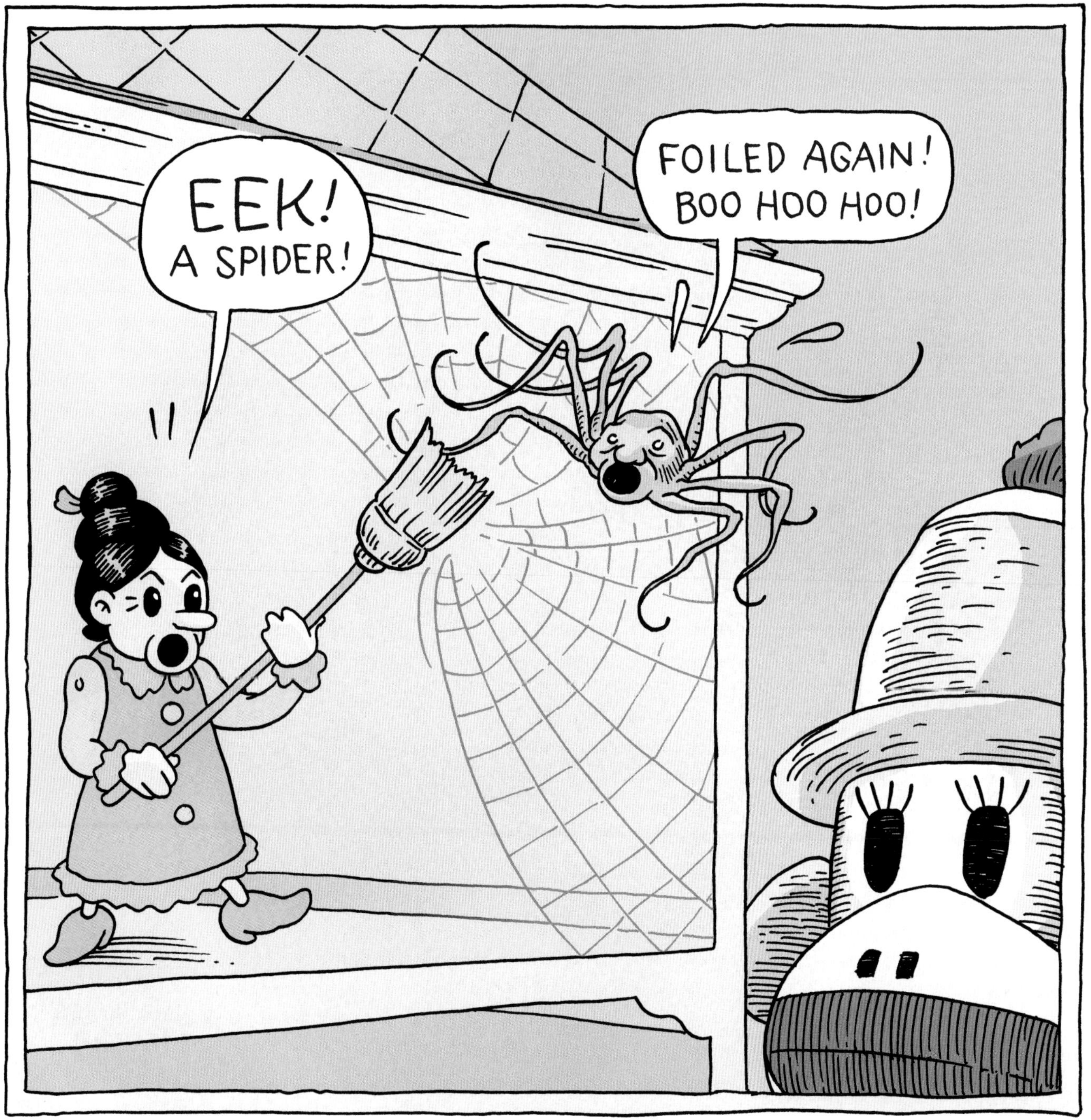
EEK! A SPIDER!
FOILED AGAIN! BOO HOO HOO!

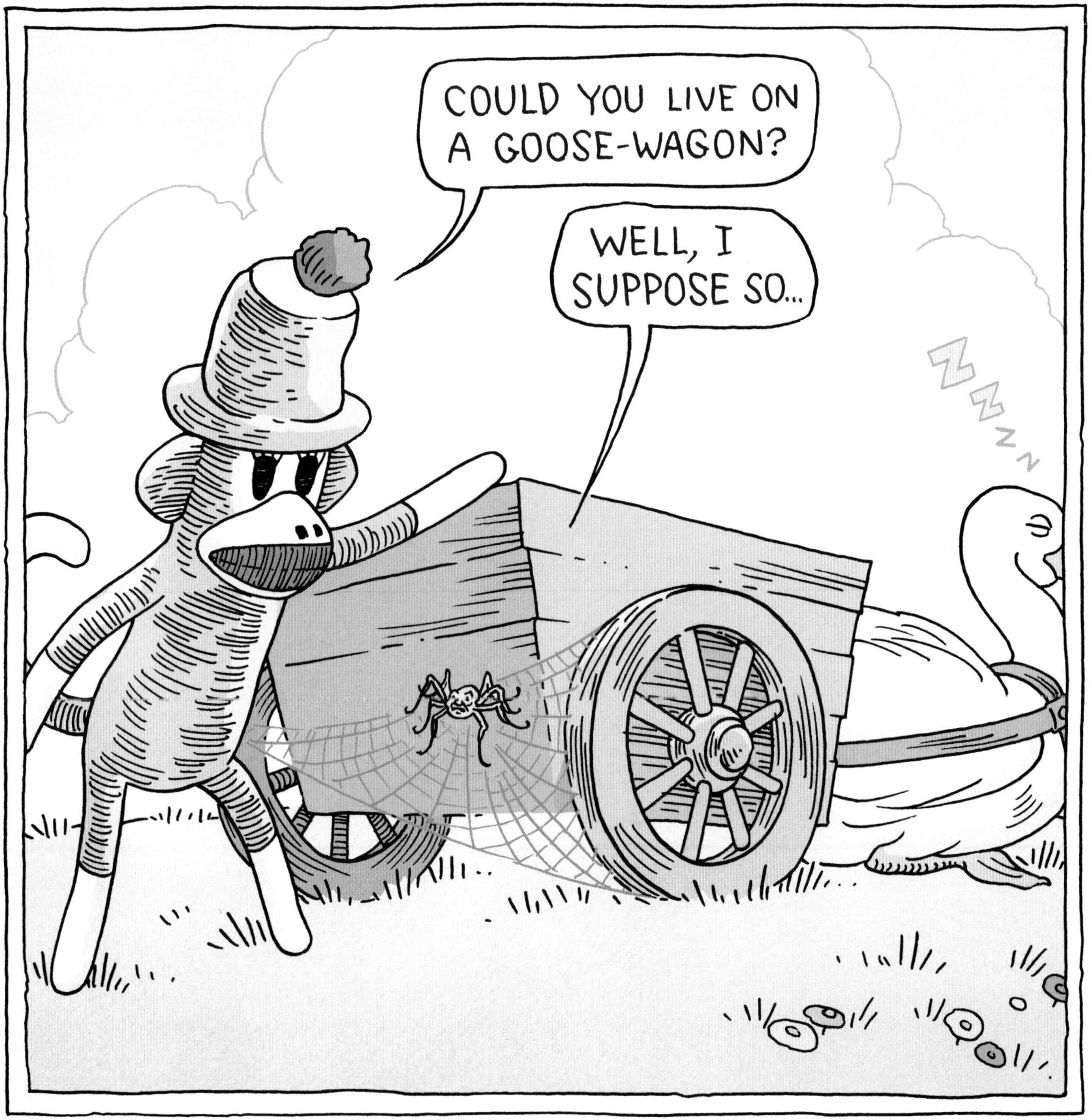
COULD YOU LIVE ON A GOOSE-WAGON?
WELL, I SUPPOSE SO...
ZZZZZ

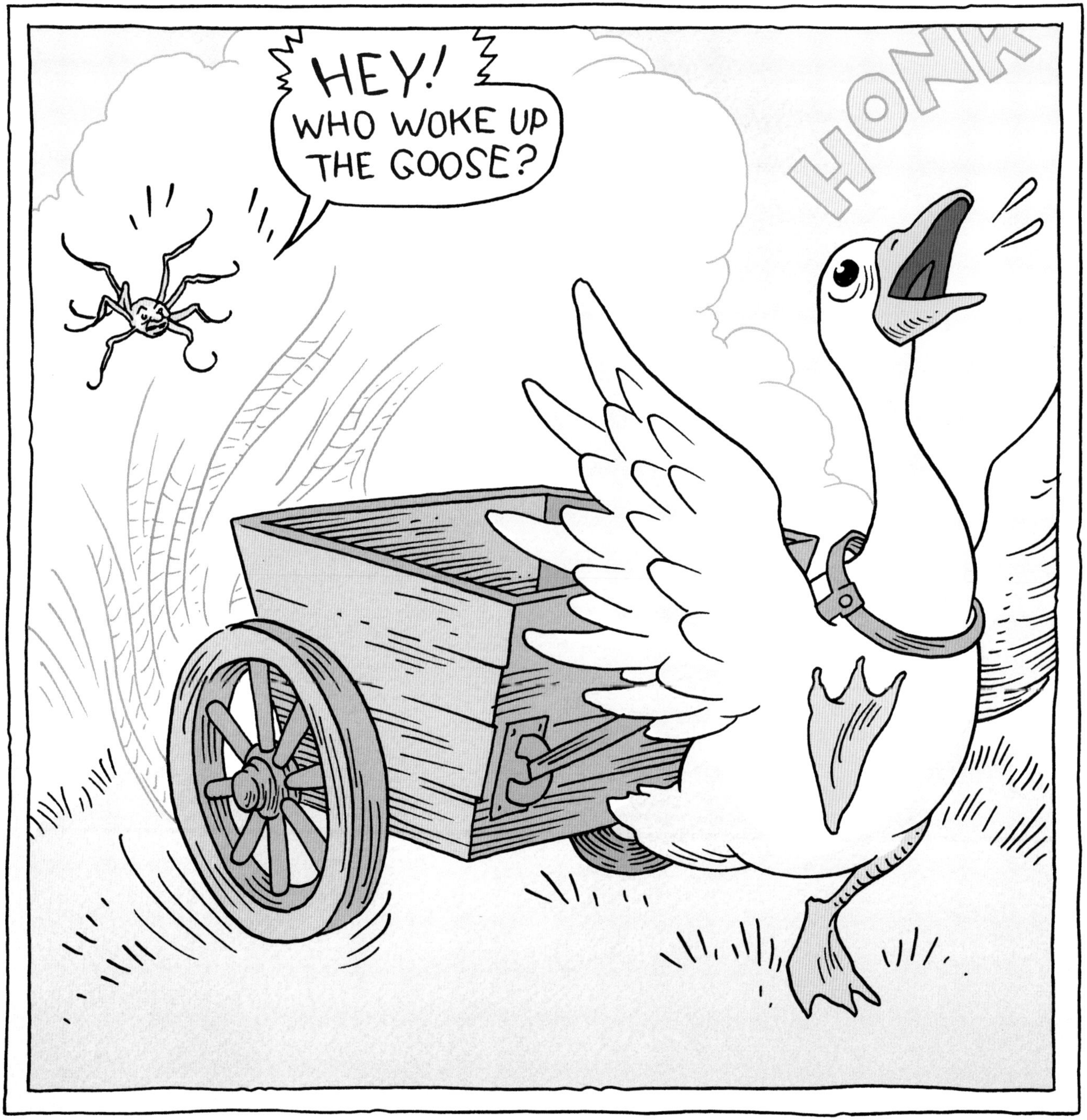
HONK
HEY!
WHO WOKE UP THE GOOSE?

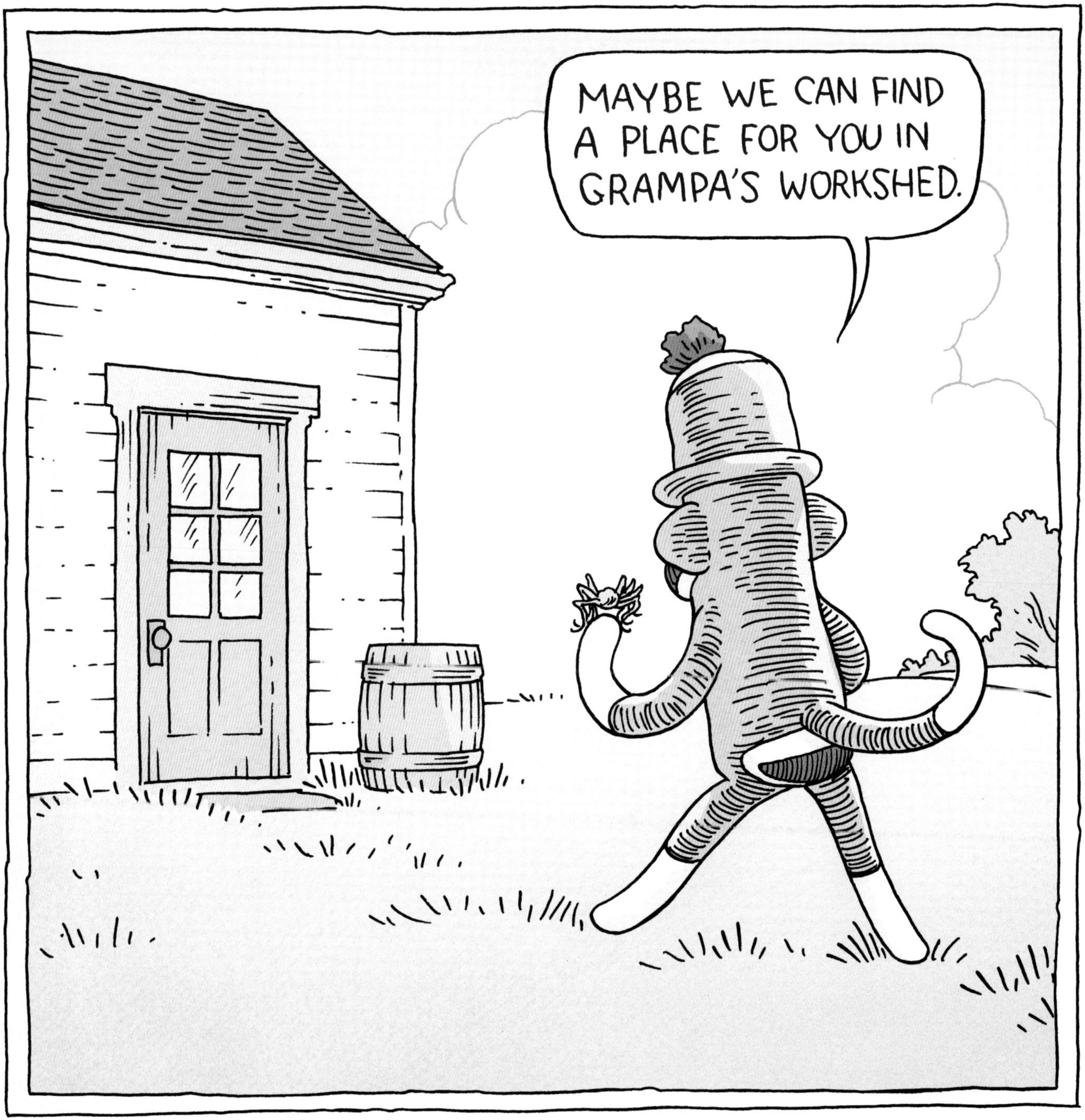
MAYBE WE CAN FIND A PLACE FOR YOU IN GRAMPA'S WORKSHED.

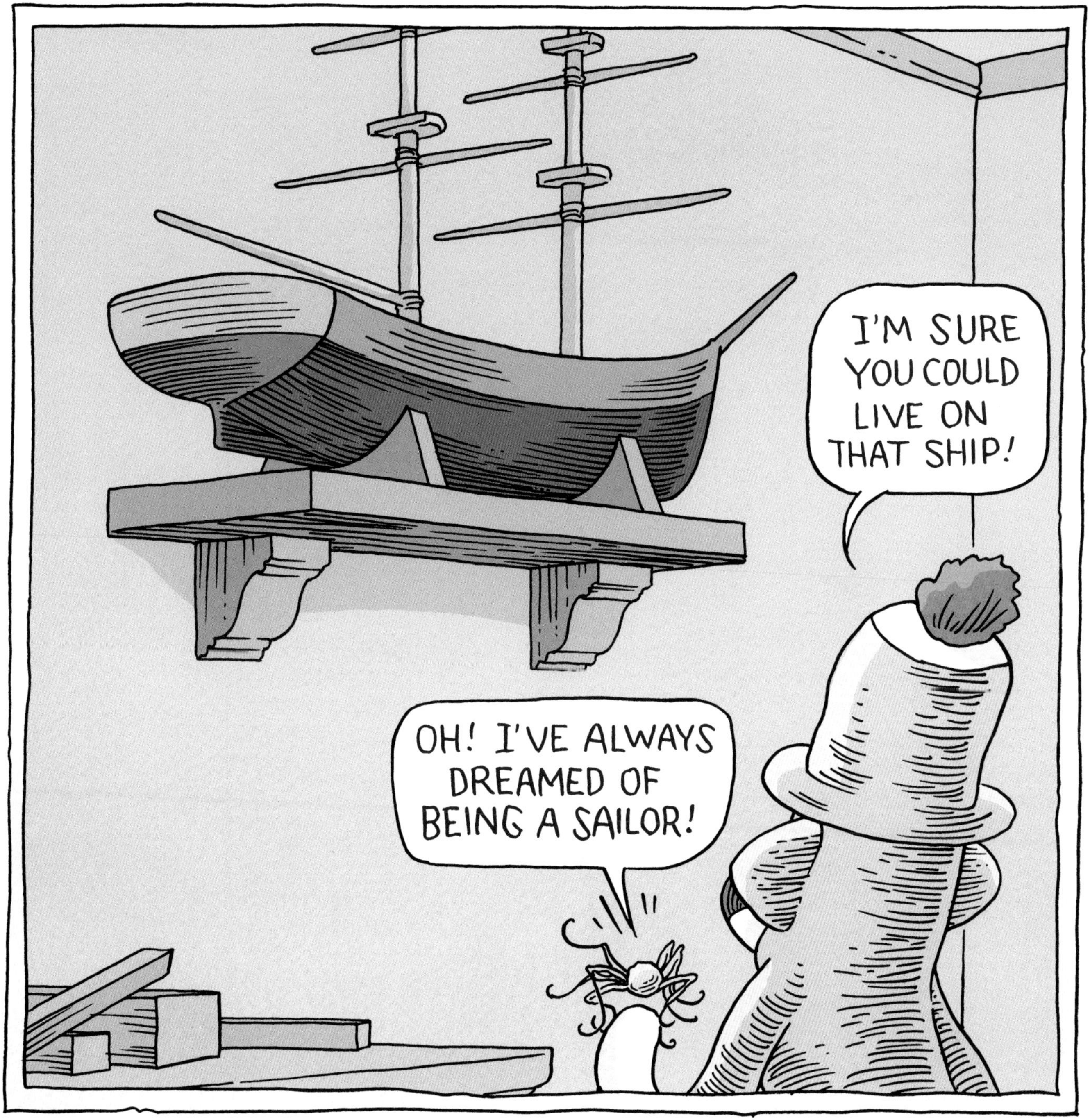
I'M SURE YOU COULD LIVE ON THAT SHIP!
OH! I'VE ALWAYS DREAMED OF BEING A SAILOR!

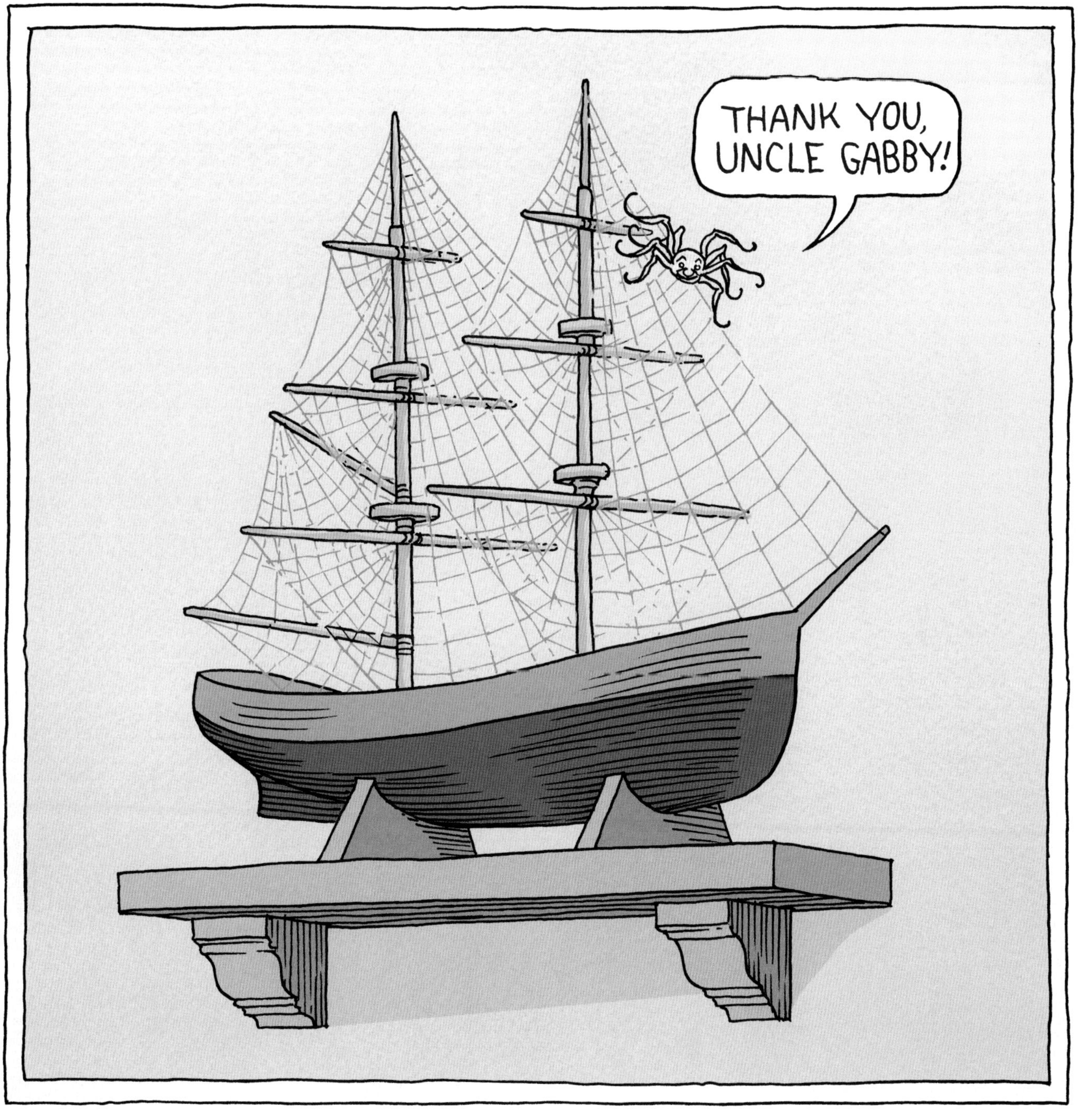
THANK YOU, UNCLE GABBY!

DESIGNER • LIA RIBAGCHI

EDITOR • DAVE LAND

PUBLISHER • MIKE RICHARDSON

LITTLE AND LARGE

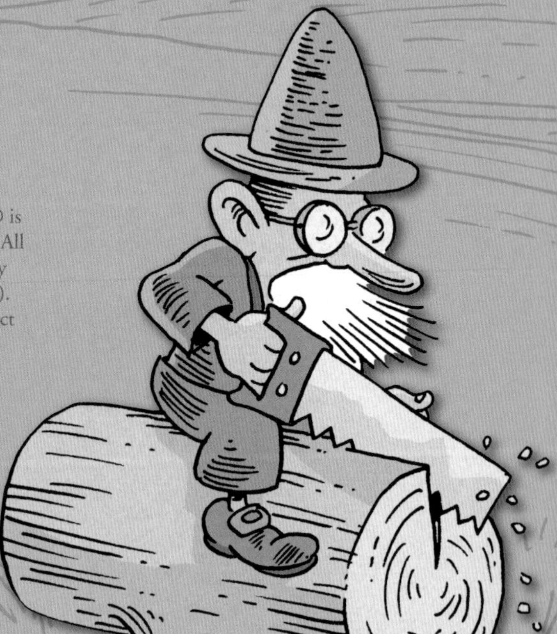

DH Press™
A division of Dark Horse Comics, Inc.
10956 SE Main Street
Milwaukie, OR 97222

First edition: September 2005
ISBN: 1-59582-010-8

10 9 8 7 6 5 4 3 2 1
PRINTED IN CHINA

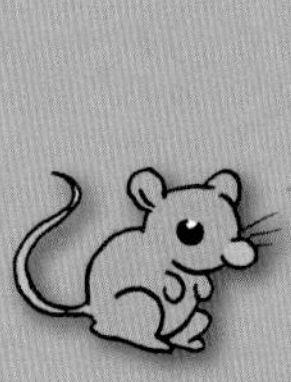